THOMAS' Train

by
The REV. W. AWDRY

SCHOLASTIC INC.

New York   Toronto   London   Auckland   Sydney
Mexico City   New Delhi   Hong Kong   Buenos Aires

Thomas often grumbled because he was not allowed to pull passenger trains.

The other engines laughed. "You're too impatient," they said. "You'd be sure to leave something behind!"

"Rubbish," said Thomas crossly. "You just wait, I'll show you."

One night, he and Henry were alone. Henry was ill. The men worked hard, but Henry didn't get better.

Now Henry usually pulled the first train in the morning, and Thomas had to get his coaches ready.

If Henry is ill, Thomas thought, perhaps I shall pull his train. Thomas ran to find the coaches.

"Come *along*. Come *along*," he fussed.

"There's plenty of time, there's plenty of time," grumbled the coaches.

He took them to the platform and wanted to run around in front at once. But his Driver wouldn't let him.

"Don't be impatient, Thomas," he said.

So Thomas waited and waited. The people got in, the Guard and Station-Master walked up and down, the porters banged the doors, and still Henry didn't come.

Thomas got more and more excited every minute.

Sir Topham Hatt came out of his office to see what was the matter. The Guard and the Station-Master told him about Henry.

"Find another engine," he ordered.

"There's only Thomas," they said.

"You'll have to do it then, Thomas. Be quick now!"

So Thomas ran around to the front and backed up to the coaches, ready to start.

"Don't be impatient," said his Driver. "Wait till everything is ready."

But Thomas was too excited to listen to a word he said.

What happened then no one knows. Perhaps they forgot to couple Thomas to the train. Perhaps Thomas was too impatient to wait till they were ready. Or perhaps his Driver pulled the lever by mistake.

Anyhow, Thomas started. People shouted and waved at him, but he didn't stop.

They're waving because I'm such a splendid engine, he thought importantly. Henry says it's hard to pull trains, but *I* think it's easy.

"Hurry! Hurry! Hurry!" he puffed, pretending to be like Gordon.

As he passed the first signal-box, he saw the men leaning out and waving and shouting.

They're pleased to see me, he thought. They've never seen me pulling a train before — it's nice of them to wave, and he whistled, "*Peep, peep,* thank you," and hurried on.

But then he came to a signal that said "Danger."

Bother! he thought. I must stop, and I was going so nicely, too. What a nuisance signals are! And he blew an angry "*peep, peep*" on his whistle.

One of the signalmen ran up. "Hullo, Thomas!" he said. "What are you doing here?"

"I'm pulling a train," said Thomas proudly. "Can't you *see?*"

"Where are your coaches, then?"

Thomas looked back. "Why bless me," he said, "if we haven't left them behind!"

"Yes," said the Signalman, "you'd better go back quickly and fetch them."

Poor Thomas was so sad he nearly cried.

"Cheer up!" said his Driver. "Let's go back quickly and try again."

At the station all the passengers were talking at once. They were telling Sir Topham Hatt, the Station-Master, and the Guard what a bad railway it was.

But when Thomas came back and they saw how sad he was, they couldn't be cross. So they coupled him to the train, and this time he *really* pulled it.

But for a long time afterward the other engines laughed at Thomas and said, "Look, there's Thomas, who wanted to pull a train, but forgot about the coaches!"

Now flip the book over to start another Thomas & Friends adventure.

THOMAS and Gordon

by
The REV. W. AWDRY

SCHOLASTIC INC.

New York   Toronto   London   Auckland   Sydney
Mexico City   New Delhi   Hong Kong   Buenos Aires

Thomas was a tank engine who lived at a big station. He had six small wheels, a short stumpy funnel, a short stumpy boiler, and a short stumpy dome.

He was a fussy little engine, always pulling coaches around. He pulled them to the station ready for the big engines to take out on long journeys. When trains came in and the people had gotten out, he would pull the empty coaches away so that the big engines could go and rest.

He was a cheeky little engine, too. He thought no engine worked as hard as he did. So he used to play tricks on the other engines. He liked best of all to come quietly beside a big engine dozing on a siding and make him jump.

"*Peep, peep, peep, pip, peep!* Wake up, lazybones!" he would whistle. "Why don't you work hard like me?"

Then he would laugh rudely and run away to find some more coaches.

One day, Gordon was resting on a siding. He was very tired. The big express he always pulled had been late, and he had to run as fast as he could to make up for lost time.

He was just going to sleep when Thomas came up in his cheeky way.

"Wake up, lazybones," he whistled. "Do some hard work for a change—you can't catch me!" And he ran off, laughing.

Instead of going to sleep again, Gordon thought about how he could pay Thomas back.

One morning, Thomas wouldn't wake up. His Driver and Fireman couldn't make him start. His fire went out and there was not enough steam.

It was nearly time for the express. The people were waiting, but the coaches weren't ready.

At last, Thomas started. "Oh, dear! Oh, dear!" he yawned.

"Come on," said the coaches. "Hurry up."

Thomas gave them a rude bump and started for the station. "Don't stop dawdling, don't stop dawdling," he grumbled.

"Where have you been? Where have you been?" asked coaches crossly.

Thomas fussed into the station where Gordon was waiting.

"*Poop, poop, poop.* Hurry up, you," said Gordon crossly.

"*Peep, pip, peep.* Hurry yourself," said cheeky Thomas.

"Yes," said Gordon, "I will." And almost before the coaches had stopped moving, Gordon came out from his siding and was coupled to the train.

"*Poop, poop,*" he whistled. "Get in quickly, please." So the people got in quickly, the signal went down, the clock struck the hour, the Guard waved his green flag, and Gordon was ready to start.

Thomas usually pushed behind the big trains to help them start. But he was always uncoupled first, so that when the train was running well, he could stop and go back.

This time he was late, and Gordon started so quickly that they forgot to uncouple Thomas.

"*Poop, poop,*" said Gordon.

"*Peep, peep, peep,*" whistled Thomas.

"Come on! Come on!" puffed Gordon to the coaches.

"Pull harder! Pull harder!" puffed Thomas to Gordon.

The heavy train slowly began to move out of the station.

The train went faster and faster—too fast for Thomas. He wanted to stop, but he couldn't.

"*Peep, peep!* Stop! Stop!" he whistled.

"Hurry, hurry, hurry," laughed Gordon in front.

"You can't get away. You can't get away," laughed the coaches.

Poor Thomas was going faster than he had ever gone before. He was out of breath and his wheels hurt him, but he had to go on.

I shall never be the same again, he thought sadly. My wheels will be quite worn out.

At last, they stopped at a station. Everyone laughed to see Thomas puffing and panting behind.

They uncoupled him, put him on a turntable, and then he ran onto a siding out of the way.

"Well, little Thomas," chuckled Gordon as he passed. "Now, you know what hard work means, don't you?"

Poor Thomas couldn't answer. He had no breath. He just puffed slowly away to rest and had a long, long drink.

He went home very slowly and was careful afterward never to be cheeky to Gordon again.

Now flip the book over to start another Thomas & Friends adventure.